LEGIBLE SCRIBBLES

A WRITER'S JOURNEY

TOSHESH MEENA

Made with ♥ on the Notion Press Platform
www.notionpress.com

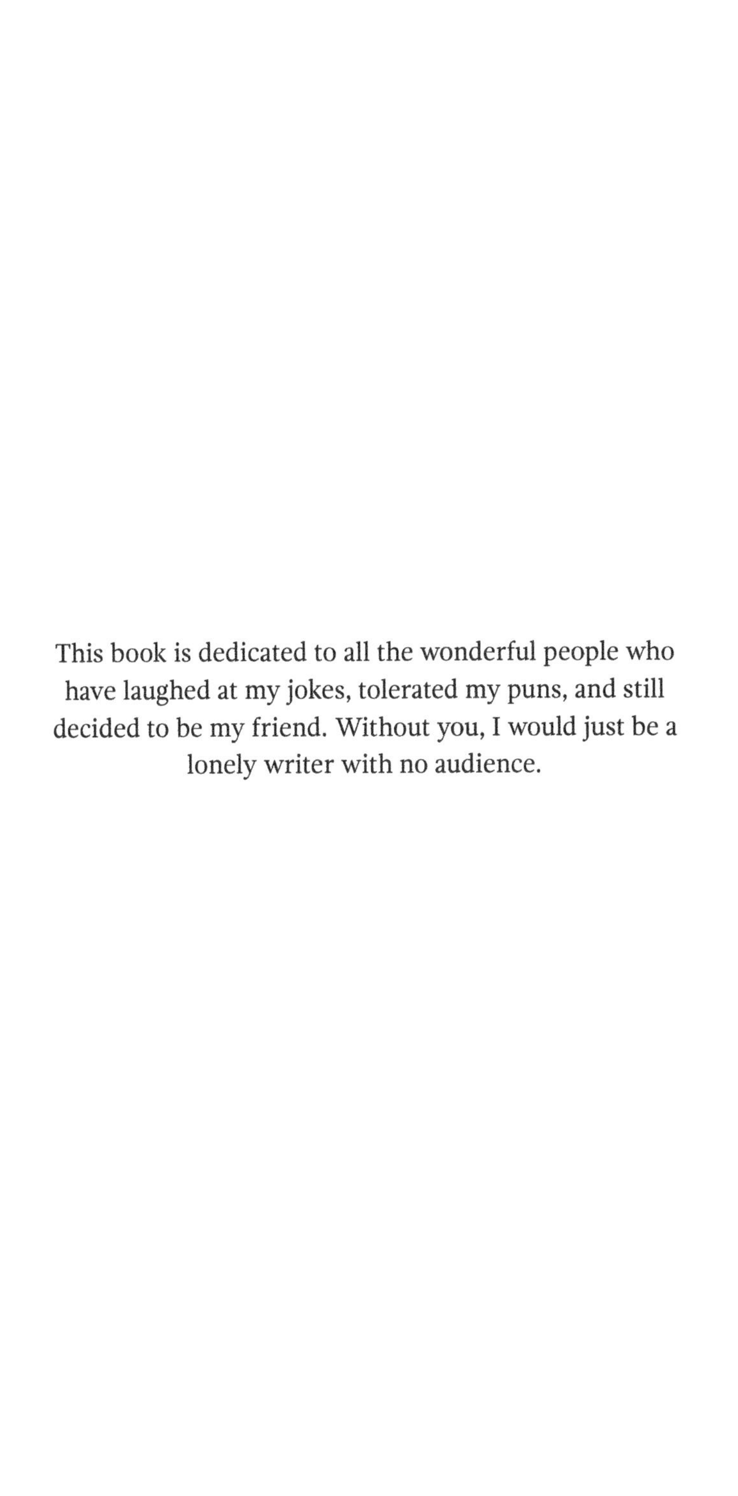

This book is dedicated to all the wonderful people who have laughed at my jokes, tolerated my puns, and still decided to be my friend. Without you, I would just be a lonely writer with no audience.

Contents

Prologue

Dear reader,

As you hold this book in your hands, I must confess something to you. This was not the book I set out to write. No, no. I had grand plans for a novel, with complex characters, intricate plotlines, and profound themes. But as it turns out, I'm not quite as talented as I thought I was. So, I settled for this book instead.

But fear not, for this book is not without its merits. You see, it's a book about a writer who can't seem to find a topic for his book. And what could be more relatable than that? So, if you're a struggling writer, or just someone who enjoys a good laugh or an absurd puzzle, then this book is for you.

And if you're wondering why I chose to write this book, well, let's just say it was either this or a book about my failure to become a successful astronaut. I think I made the right choice.

So, without further ado, let's dive into the world of writing, doubts, and legacy. And who knows? Maybe by the end of this book, you'll be inspired to write a book of your own. Or at the very least, you'll have a good chuckle.

CHAPTER I

Snails, Trees, and Clouds

Bright sunshine and a refreshing wind made this one of the best days of the year. However, the mood of a stormy night permeated his apartment. He sat at his desk, idly staring at the empty pages in front of him with a blank expression. Thinking about why it was so hard for him to put together a simple story. As his mind started to wander, he looked up from the paper and towards the window. The magnificent sight outside the window brought on an unexpected wave of nostalgia.

He had always been enamoured with stories, even as a young child. He was in awe of the fantastical settings and characters that authors created, as well as the intricate stories they wove and the feelings they evoked. Having the freedom to invent his own universe and populate it with his own characters before publishing it for the world to enjoy was an attractive prospect. He had long wished he could express himself on paper. Commit his ideas and emotions to paper. Unfortunately, he discovered the hard way that desires alone aren't always sufficient.

His love of stories grew as he got older, and he began devouring books to the point of immersing himself in them while daydreaming about what it would be like to write stories as captivating and exciting as the ones he was reading. He'd spend hours jotting down notes and fragments of stories in notebooks, chronicling the exploits of his invented people. His literary efforts usually resulted in a jumbled mess of ink on paper, but he gave them his all nonetheless in the hopes that someday they might resonate with readers and elicit some sort of intellectual or emotional connection from them.

His mind was filled with recollections of the past as he sat in his room and looked out the window at the bustling metropolis below. This was not the first time he had been forced into a situation where he had trouble both thinking of and expressing an idea. Now that he has some distance, he realises that all this occurred during a period when he was still oblivious to the correlation between his development as a writer and his own personal growth. Writing a story was indeed a constant battle because it required him to understand himself and make sense of a reality that often seemed paradoxical. He didn't realise then that the road ahead would be littered with challenges. Challenges that would test his resolve and, in the process, drive him mad.

In the beginning, all he had to do was decide on a plot idea. Despite its seeming simplicity, this assignment would take him on an experience of a lifetime. For a long time, he couldn't make up his mind; he felt as if he was swimming aimlessly in an infinite sea of ideas and alternatives.

He used to spend hours, if not days, contemplating the most absurd and nonsensical notions. For example, he once thought about attempting to write out what a tree may be thinking. From this giant's high perch, he could see the whole world and learn more about the treasures below. This made him very interested. In the end, though, he determined that the tree was happy where it was and didn't need any disturbances. Refraining from bothering the tree, he chose to observe a snail slithering around the tree's roots. One idea he had was to relate the adventures of a snail. Again, the potential of following this slow creature on its trip and deciphering the obstacles it encounters grabbed his attention. Sad to say, the unexpected awareness of how long it had been since he had gone on any adventure of his own had unearthed some unwelcome frustration, so he let the snail go on its own adventure. A good time should be had by at least one of them, he thought. At that point, his attention went away from the snail and towards the sky, where he entertained ideas of penning an article about the daily life of clouds. He was interested in the symbolic undercurrents of these transient shapes. Soon, though, he realised that the clouds were content where they were and that it may be best to leave them where they were. These are just a few of the many possibilities he considered while hunting for the perfect story idea. It seemed at that time that the hunt would never stop.

CHAPTER II

Great Squirrel Invasion

The minutes became hours, the hours became days, and the days became weeks. When he looked at the calendar, he realised that several weeks had passed in what seemed like a blink of an eye, yet his story had only progressed to a few legible scribbles. As time went on, he became increasingly frustrated with his lack of progress and started focusing more on his everyday activities. On occasion, though, the nagging urge to put pen to paper would return, and he'd feel frustrated once more. His frustration with the situation, already thick enough to cut with a dull pencil, grew during these lulls.

By this point in his life, he had read enough books to fill a modest collection. He had engaged in conversations with other writers until he was blue in the face and had gone to so many writing workshops that the experience would have worn out a marathon runner. Yet, nothing seemed to click. His lists of potential titles, epic arcs, and character descriptions were extensive. There were a million and one ideas floating around in his head, but none of them felt right. Nothing he tried seemed perfect, no matter how many story ideas he came up with. There was the beginning of a story dormant in each scribble in his notebook, just waiting to be unearthed, but he couldn't seem to get the creative juices to flow.

One day, he was fortunate enough to cross paths with a friend who happened to be a talented author. He sought his advice. One of his nuggets of wisdom was to choose a topic that really engaged him. Simple as pie, right? No, not really.

With a mind full of fiction and an attention span as fickle as the wind, how does one choose just one idea to pursue amidst the vast sea of possibilities?

As he strolled homeward, deep in conversation with his buddy, an electrifying notion jolted him: his mundane routine was stifling his creative flow. It was as if a light bulb had flickered to life above his head, illuminating the need for change in his life. The unvarying nature of his days had seeped into his psyche, causing his imagination to wither and wane. It was time for a shake-up, a seismic shift, to reignite the spark of his inner fire. So, choosing to take gradual steps towards it, he went for a leisurely stroll the next day to the public library in his neighbourhood. All geared up and ready to indulge his inner bibliophile. He reasoned that somewhere, with so many books on so many topics, there must be a treasure trove of ideas that would surprise and delight him.

He noticed as he browsed the shelves that several of the books were not in the order he had last seen them. He couldn't recall seeing them before, but they appeared out of place. He brushed it aside and began looking, only to find that the more he browsed, the more volumes were misplaced. His wonder about whether or not the library was undergoing renovation caused him to stop. To have his suspicions confirmed, he walked over to the librarian's desk and asked what was going on. Her eyes sparkled as she told him that a squirrel army had taken over. It seems that they mistook the library for a warehouse full of plush bedding, causing quite a ruckus in their quest for the most comfortable beds. The ridiculousness of the circumstance made him unable to contain his laughter, and he couldn't help but laugh out loud. This certainly looks like an inspiration for a Kafkaesque tale. He decided to take the bull by the horns and write a story about several squirrels that invade a library and end up becoming librarians. He sat down at his desk, ready to write, his quills twitching with excitement, only to realise he had no clue how to devise a squirrel story. With regard to squirrels, he was as clueless as a rock. A vengeful mood returned as he stared blankly at the empty pages in front of him. He tried to put pen to paper with a few additional possibilities, but nothing stuck. There didn't seem to be a way out of the creative rut he was in.

He was still set on shaking things up, but this time he would take a more adventurous path. He went on a little trip to the countryside for some much-needed R&R in the great outdoors. His vacation consisted of long, introspective sitting by a river and gorgeous hikes in the surrounding countryside, but his true motivations were less altruistic.

During his walk along the riverbank, he discovered a rabbit's playground. These rabbits were skipping and hopping about like they didn't care that he was there. Their innocence was both endearing and inspiring, making him want to write a story about bunny adventures. Thrilled, he hurried home to start writing. Yet as he started, the realisation dawned on him that he knew jackrabbit about the lifestyle or habitat of rabbits. That's not once, but twice on the same day. The agony of being completely clueless for the second time in a day quickly diminished his excitement. Sigh, the joys of being a clueless writer.

CHAPTER III

The Chair that Stole My Muse

As he tried in vain to compose and, more crucially, finish a story, he ran against a myriad of hurdles that made writing a story seem like a Herculean undertaking. It started to take its toll on him, as exhaustion crept up on him. This exhaustion grew over time, manifesting itself in a plethora of explanations that became progressively puzzling and devoid of logic.

For instance, one morning he couldn't write anything and blamed it all on the chair he was sitting on. He claimed that the chair's smooth armrest and sturdy structure taunted him. It seemed as though it were saying, "You won't be able to compose in me." He gave up and proceeded to the living room couch, only to discover that it was too appealing with its comfy cushions, smooth fabric, and inviting backrest. He momentarily came to the silly conclusion that the furnishings were the only reason he couldn't write.

The next day, he found himself complaining about the ambience. He remarked that the setting was either too quiet or too loud for him. It was either too hot or too humid. There was either too little or too much breeze. Nothing seemed to calm his overly sensitive senses, and he felt utterly powerless. Then there was the time he grumbled about the pen he was using not wanting to do its job. "You're just not the pen for me," he said under his breath as he put the pen down and grabbed up another. He looked like a knight on the hunt for the ideal sword, but all he found were dull uninspiring blades.

His explanation that his canine friend was impeding his progress was perhaps the stupidest one he'd ever come up with. Despite the dog's calm stance, he found it impossible to concentrate anytime he was in his presence. As the man would motion for his dog to go, the animal would only yawn and ball up in response. That's when he would feel a momentary sensation that he'd just reached the bottom of the barrel at that point. In his effort to find an external cause for his own failure to write, he didn't rule out the sun, the moon, or the stars. "Maybe the planets aren't properly aligned," he would often whisper, accusing the universe of working against him. There were only a few sporadic instances in which he attributed his lack of artistic progress to something on the inside. His sloppy handwriting was usually to blame. "These letters are just too wobbly," he'd whine as if his shaky handwriting was the source of all his problems. Not to mention the ever-popular "writer's block" justification. As if inspiration could be followed and caught like a butterfly, he repeatedly declared, "It's just not coming to me." But it felt like he could never quite get a hold of it; it was always just a few inches beyond his grasp.

This made him chuckle at himself, since who else but he could be so completely ridiculous? All his difficulties and explanations boiled down to one thing: he was a captive of his own thoughts as he was stuck in a vicious loop.

He was having a hard time getting started with writing, but it was even harder for him to come up with a good idea for his story. He used to spend hours, if not days, thinking about the most bizarre and ridiculous themes. There was a time when he wondered about investigating the mysterious pasts of inanimate items. Curious about what mysteries were behind the walls and in the stuff surrounding him, he was completely enthralled but after some consideration, however, he decided that this would not be the most fascinating topic and that perhaps it would be best to leave the artefacts shrouded in mystery. A broad range of such themes, some credible and others plain ludicrous, were explored by him. All of them would eventually lead to the same conclusion of not being good enough and then just evaporating in the air. The ideas he had generated from these quirky themes would vanish as quickly as they came to him, leaving him with nothing but a dry piece of paper with few ink stains on it.

CHAPTER IV

When Your Brain Takes a Vacation

After months of being bombarded by an endless stream of obstacles, he found himself sinking into a pit of self-doubt. From selecting a topic to creating content for it, he had made so little progress that the idea of finishing a narrative one day felt like a pipe dream. Words continued eluding him, and he began to doubt his ability as a writer and his place in the world of literary arts.

One Sunday afternoon, as the fan above gently swirled, he sat on his bed seriously considering his situation. After encountering a plethora of others, some of which were utterly absurd and others less so, he had stumbled upon an introspective idea. In addition to being reflective in nature, it also appeared to be a starting point for something original.

His need to polish every word of his work had turned into a hindrance, and his fixation on finding the ideal phrasing had caused him to lose sight of the spark of creativity that lay at the heart of his writing. For the first time, he had actually realised that this journey of writing a book might also be as rewarding as the finished result. He didn't know why, but following that, he couldn't stop reminiscing about that excursion to the countryside and the enigmatic events that transpired that day. Then, it dawned on him that the struggle to write a book was a story in itself and a hilarious one at that! Finally, a much-awaited stroke of genius.

Immediately, he realised that he was doing everything wrong. Rather than wasting time trying to explore and write about obscure topics, he decided to draw inspiration from his own experiences instead. Who wouldn't want to read about the tribulations of a writer who just can't seem to write?

It seemed like a fascinating notion where the writer would have written a tale about not being able to write one - how meta is that?

After having a stroke of brilliance that would have turned even the most intelligent owl on the block green with envy, the veil was finally pulled back, and all of a sudden, he had a plan. He would spill all of the behind-the-scenes details about the highs and lows, the in-betweens, and everything else that comes with being a writer who is both passionate and clueless. It would be a wild ride filled with hardships, fears, doubts, and aspirations, and he was too eager to take everyone on this rollercoaster of a ride. He couldn't wait to take everyone on this rollercoaster of a ride. A story of a daring adventurer on a mission to find their voice, conquer their fears, uncover their innermost thoughts and emotions, and dig up some semblance of purpose in their artistic endeavours. It would be a story that encompassed more than simply his own experiences, but at the same time, it would be deeply ingrained in his one-of-a-kind personality.

Never in a million years would he have guessed that all of the time and effort he put into trying to find the perfect story would ultimately pay off and reward him with one. It was an adventure in and of itself, replete with a mountain of unexpected turns and oddities. It had morphed into the kind of trip of which he would always reminisce gratefully and with a touch of sarcasm. The absurdity of his own troubles was not lost on him, and he started to see the humour in it as soon as he started to formulate a haphazardly laid out strategy for what to write in it and how to write it. With that, he started the next leg of his journey: actually writing the story.

His passion for storytelling, his voracious curiosity, and the emotional whirlwind that swirled around inside of him were the driving elements behind his desire to work as a writer. He started to feel like he was looking for something deeper, a connection to the world and to himself. He had just realized once again that writing isn't just about scribbling words on a page, it's a wild goose chase for self-awareness. It's a method for him to understand who he is, confront his fears head-on, and let his thoughts and emotions soar through the air like a kite with a message attached to the end of its string. All the while, using his own especially wobbly handwriting to chronicle it.

He jolted himself awake and jumped out of bed, with the sensation that a burden had been removed from his shoulders. Gone was the pressure to find the perfect story, and in its stead came the urge to express his experiences with other folks. He was no longer simply a writer; rather, he was a storyteller who possessed a story of his own. And believe him when he said that this tale would be one for the record books. Put on your seatbelts, folks, because you're in for a bumpy journey!

As he sauntered towards his writing gear, he finally acknowledged it for what it truly was: a scintillating diamond concealed in plain view. The monotony of daily life was suddenly infused with new excitement, as he began discovering the beauty in the banal.

CHAPTER V

Writer's Block: A Battle of Wits

Now that he had a premise for his story, he was excited to get started with actually writing it. To his dismay, he would soon discover that his trials were only beginning. As he began working on his story, he ran into a lot of impediments he hadn't counted on.

As a result of these totally unexpected bumps in the road, he was plagued by severe self-doubt. Just the idea of having to write about his hardships for the story felt unnerving, and he was filled with the fear that he wouldn't be able to approach the content of the story sensibly. The fear that what he said would fall short of expressing the full extent of his agony rendered him paralyzed. Writing, he told himself, is not about winning people over so much as it is about recording his own thoughts and experiences for posterity. With this insight in hand, he seemed to be capable of pushing through his doubts and keep on writing.

An unexpected challenge arose as he kept working on his story. In the process of writing about this topic, he became immersed in his own head and could not pull out. He was acutely conscious of the problems he experienced, and he was unable to find an escape from them. It was problematic since he found it hard to write dispassionately about his experiences because of how deeply involved he was. Nonetheless, he was resolved to get through this challenge, so he made an active effort to detach himself emotionally from the difficulty and write dispassionately about it.

Deficiency in creativity was a problem he had to deal with. There were instances when he couldn't put his feelings into words because his mind was blank. When he was having trouble, he questioned whether or not his struggles were destined to be chronicled. But at the other hand, he was aware that writing is rarely a straightforward process and that he would inevitably run into roadblocks. He was resolved to find a way through this roadblock, so he distracted his attention from writing and spent some time doing something else that stimulated his mind.

To finally be able to put pen to paper required a lot of hard work and patience on his part, but he was eventually successful in overcoming the challenges that kept appearing in his path. Over time, he developed the skill of writing dispassionately about his trials, and he was finally able to do justice to the depth of his experiences. When he finally got around to putting his thoughts on paper, he felt a tremendous sense of relief and pleasure in having overcome his issues. An insignificant victory in the grand scheme of things, but one that means a lot to the one who achieved it. He had succeeded in making something worthwhile out of his silly hardships, something that might be shared with others. From these fires of writer's despair, he rose, ready to tell the world about his adventures.

CHAPTER VI

The Day My Pen Became My Worst Enemy

Despite the slow pace, he was pleased with the progress he was making with his story. A strange feeling, though, would occasionally invade his consciousness. It felt as if he had gotten lost in the middle of a dense jungle and was wandering about in circles, hoping to locate the exit. The trees and bushes seemed to be closing in on him, making it difficult to see his surroundings.

He was looking for some semblance of hope in the empty pieces of paper in front of him. The task of brainstorming possibilities for this story was starting to feel like a battle. To make matters worst, the words he had once trusted as friends turned out to be his adversaries, leaving him with a feeling of loss. His battle against the words, his new foes, felt doomed.

The longer this went on, the more he felt like he was sinking into a bottomless pit of frustration and disillusionment. The deeper he went, the more difficult it was to claw his way back to the surface. He couldn't find the coast amid a sea of doubt.

As the days, weeks, and months wore on, he lost more and more zest for writing. His inner fervour had begun to wane as the pressures of daily life took precedence. Work, the stresses of daily life, and the monotony of the daily grind had him completely worn out. To-do lists and worry flooded his thoughts, preventing creative thinking. The world around him appeared to be moving faster and faster, and he tried to keep up. Once peaceful intervals, during which he could sit down and write, were suddenly cluttered with distractions. Yes, he had a lot on his plate, but he was also mentally and physically drained. To him, it was like being on a treadmill and being unable to slow down or stop. His life became so hectic that he hardly had any spare moments for introspection.

To a large extent, he had stopped thinking about writing. What had fueled him no longer did, and he was left feeling hollow and dissatisfied. But at the same time, he was happy, happy with the ordinariness of his existence and the predictability of his days.

The story's pages turned yellow and brittle as a result of his reluctance to see the adventure through to its end. The writer he once was had given way to the guy who simply existed from day to day. And in this, he experienced a weird satisfaction, the comfort of knowing that his journey as a writer was over and that he could now focus on the adventure of life itself. The journey had become a burden, and he was glad to be done with it at the time.

Thus, it stands to reason that he never had a story released and distributed to a mass audience. Despite his best efforts, he was never able to pursue a future in writing. But he was content in the knowledge that his path had been unique and instructive in many ways. Ultimately, he learned to value the journey as much as, if not more than, the outcome.

CHAPTER VII

The Day I Tried to Make a Fancy Dinner and Ended up Ordering Pizza Instead

Now, after many years, only memories and experiences of this journey remain for him. He was carried along the river of life like a leaf drifting down the river. With the hustle and bustle of life taking centre stage, the journey of writing a story had slipped backstage. But all of that was before he recently came upon a box that was dusty and covered in spiderwebs as he was cleaning his bookshelves. There were notebooks and compositions in it from years past, including the one he had spent countless hours on but never finished.

As soon as he opened the box, the odour of mouldy paper and faded ink filled his nostrils. He picked up the first notebook and started reading, but it made him feel weird like he was reading the journal of a total stranger. Like a jigsaw puzzle with too many parts missing, the words made no sense and were all over the place. Initially, he thought quite highly of the quality of his work. Sad to say, he can only see its flaws now, like a man looking at his reflection in a broken mirror.

He continued on to the next notebook, then the one after that, each one reflecting his younger self's aspirations, disappointments, and eventual growth. He thought back on the nights he'd spent crying into the paper, the hours he'd spent daydreaming, and the frustration and disappointment he'd felt when the words just wouldn't come.

He came upon a passage that made him reminisce as he browsed through the pages. The focus of the text was on getting there, rather than arriving. For a brief moment, he was taken back to when he believed that the process of writing itself was more important than the finished product. He had learned to appreciate the beauty of the process and to find joy in the act of writing, regardless of whether or not the words were perfect. His time as an aspiring writer had been one of self-discovery, of learning to be honest with himself and to accept his limitations.

As he continued to read, he found himself getting more and more engrossed by the story he had created. The characters came alive for him once more on the pages, their trials and tribulations striking a chord within him. And before he realized it, the enthusiasm that had once inspired him to create had him rewriting, revising, and editing.

It was like a dam had broken, and the words were pouring out of his pen. In retrospect, he can see how much he has progressed as a communicator over the years. His intended objective of cleaning his bookshelves had long since been forgotten as he grew preoccupied with the writing process. This time, he was able to complete in a few hours what would have taken him many months to do before. And before he knew it, he was already down to the last few sentences of his story. It was on this day that he, years after beginning one, completed one.

Despite its flaws, it was uniquely his and a reflection of his experience. He paused and took a few deep breaths. After finishing the story and being pleased with how it turned out, he made the decision to release it on the internet so that other people would perhaps read it. Sharing it with others first made him hesitant. But it would seem that he had indeed matured over these years since he swiftly overcame that hesitancy and went forward with the release.

When early reactions to his tale started trickling in, he experienced a range of emotions. On the one hand, he was ecstatic that people liked his story, and that they related to the characters and the path he had created. On the other hand, he felt vulnerable, knowing that his words were being scrutinized and his tale was being examined and studied.

Just like a kid on his first day of school, he read the evaluations with equal parts eagerness to learn and apprehension about what could lie ahead. Quite a few of the reviews were effusive in their compliments, describing his short tale as a fascinating work. However, there were some who were more judgmental, who pointed out its many defects and failings and highlighted all of its rough spots. Accordingly, he learned to see any critique, positive or negative, as a step along the route.

For so many years, he had been immersed in his tale, and now, as the reviews began to come in, he felt as if a part of his existence was drawing to a conclusion. He had lived and breathed his story. He felt bittersweet pleasure while reading them. He felt that the story's reception—both good and bad—was indicative of the strength of his words and the work he put into capturing his experience. At the same time, he was overwhelmed by the knowledge that his time as a writer was drawing to a close.

He had his doubts, but in the end, he realized that it had all been worthwhile. He had grown so much as a person and expanded his understanding of the world, and he had made something that would last as a symbol of the value of hard work and the charm of the trip.

After that lengthy detour, he found his way back to the shelves of books. After giving it a good cleaning and rearranging, he went ahead and sealed Pandora's box, feeling a sense of relief and contentment. This trip is over, but the lessons he's learned along the way will be with him always, like echoes carried on the breeze. And like a traveller coming home, he would treasure those recollections, knowing that they had helped form him into the person he is now. Therefore, he re-shelved the box, not to serve as a constant reminder of something that remained undone, but rather as a symbol of his journey, an experience for which he will be eternally thankful.

Printed by Libri Plureos GmbH in Hamburg,
Germany